Written by Keith West

Illustrated by Abigail Marble

CHARACTERS

SCENE 1

(Dana's new to Deepvale School. She notices Sophie, Anna and Jade. They're sitting in the classroom, having arrived early. She walks nervously up to them.)

DANA: *(shyly)* Hi.

SOPHIE: *(turning round to look at Dana)* Hi. What are you doing in our classroom? You new here?

DANA: Yes, I'm Dana. I've just arrived here – we've just moved in. What's your name?

SOPHIE: My name's Sophie and my mates are Anna *(pointing to the other girl)* and Jade.

ANNA: You can sit with us if you like.

(Sophie scowls.)

DANA: *(enthusiastically)* Thanks!

SOPHIE: I can tell you're not from round here. You're different.

DANA: Mum and I have just moved into Wordsworth Crescent.

SOPHIE: *(smirking)* Wordsworth Crescent?

JADE: Isn't that where Natalie Shanks lives?

SOPHIE: *(nastily)* Longshanks, sheepshanks.
(to Dana) She's weird. We don't like people from
Wordsworth Crescent, *(to Jade and Anna)* do we?

(Dana looks nervous and swallows hard.)

JADE: No.

ANNA: We don't.

SOPHIE: *(pointing at Dana's clothes)* Why aren't you in school uniform, like us? I wouldn't be seen dead in what you're wearing.

(Dana looks down at her clothes.)

JADE: *(nastily)* Yeah, what's so special about you? Why do you have to be different?

DANA: Because –

JADE: Because you're from Wordsworth Crescent, that's why. They're all nerds down that part of town.

DANA: *(upset)* No … I …

(Sophie and Jade laugh. Anna looks at Dana with a hint of sympathy.)

SOPHIE: What did you and your mates do at your old school? Play sports or anything? We play sports down at the big field on Saturdays.

DANA: We used to do drama. There was a drama club at ...

JADE: *(bored)* We don't play games.

DANA: Drama isn't just playing games ...

SOPHIE: Could have fooled us, eh, Jade? *(to Jade, indicating Dana)* Just like Natalie!

JADE: *(smirking)* What?

SOPHIE: She's like Natalie ... you know ... funny.

DANA: *(worried)* Don't you do drama? It's really good fun.

(The three girls shake their heads.)

DANA: I don't *have* to do drama. It's just ... that's what we did at our old school.

SOPHIE: *(mocking)* A school for funny people.

ANNA: *We* talk about clothes, fashion, pop stars, music ... that kind of stuff.

DANA: *(trying to smile)* That's cool. I like talking too. I like fashion.

JADE: *(pointing at Dana's clothes)* Looks like it!

(Jade and Sophie laugh.)

SOPHIE: *(to Anna and Jade)* Come on, let's go next door. We'll see Brad and his mates. *(glaring at Dana)* They must be funny where *she* comes from. She speaks in a silly way.

DANA: But –

SOPHIE: *(to Anna)* They must breed people like Natalie where *she* comes from.

(The three girls walk out of the room, leaving Dana alone. She looks down at the table and puts her head in her hands.)

SCENE 2

(Dana arrives home. Her mum is in the kitchen, unpacking a bag of groceries.)

MUM: *(cheerfully)* How was school, Dana?

DANA: *(quietly)* OK.

MUM: I'm dying for a cuppa. Want something to drink, love?

(Dana shakes her head.)

MUM: Did you like your new teacher?

DANA: Mrs Croxley's OK.

MUM: *(brightly)* Everything went well then?

DANA: Suppose so.

(Mum puts the kettle on to boil.)

MUM: What did you do?

(Dana picks up the TV remote.)

DANA: Oh, this and that.

MUM: Do they have a drama club at the new school?

DANA: No. Anyway, I don't like drama any more. I like talking about music, fashion, you know ...

MUM: Anything wrong, Dana? You used to love drama.

DANA: It's just games.

MUM: Well, I'm cooking a nice tea ... salmon, your favourite.

DANA: I'm not hungry. I don't want anything.

MUM: *(worried)* Are you sure you're OK?

(Dana nods.)

MUM: Made any new friends?

DANA: Yes ... Sophie, Jade and Anna. They're really nice.

MUM: Good. You would tell me if there was anything upsetting you, wouldn't you? Do you want to help me cook? I know you like cooking.

DANA: *(shaking her head)* I've got some artwork to do – there's an art competition. Mrs Croxley told us about it and there are posters up all over school, it's quite a big thing. *(brightening up)* I could win it if I work hard.

MUM: Great, what's the project?

DANA: We have to make a collage ... on anything we like. I had this idea to do something about our new street, showing why it's so much nicer than our old place.

MUM: That's a great idea.

DANA: I'm going to get started.

(Dana leaves the kitchen.)

SCENE 3

(The next day, Dana's sitting alone in the school playground. Natalie walks up to her and sits down.)

NATALIE: *(quietly)* You're the new girl?

DANA: Yes.

NATALIE: I know you live near me. I just thought I'd say hello. I know what it's like to be new.

DANA: It's all right, I'm sure it'll be fine – once everyone gets to know me.

NATALIE: When I first arrived, I was friends with Anna ... but Sophie was jealous. She and Jade got Anna and threatened her. They spread these stories about me and … I tried to stand up to them, but it made things worse, so I just keep away from them – it's easier that way.

DANA: But that's not fair.

NATALIE: It's just the way it is. Look, I've got to go, I've got a doctor's appointment this afternoon, so I won't be around, but – just don't let them get to you.

DANA: *(smiling)* I won't. Honestly, Natalie – I'm fine, but thanks.

(Natalie leaves.)

(Anna walks up to Dana and sits down next to her.)

ANNA: How're things?

DANA: *(smiling)* OK I guess.

ANNA: Just keep your head down and don't annoy Sophie. Then she'll let you in. She's scared anyone will take us away from her. When she gets to know you, she'll be OK.

DANA: But Natalie's not been let in.

ANNA: *(whispering)* Don't hang around with Natalie, OK? Sophie's never forgiven her for standing up to her in front of everyone, and she's never going to like anyone for hanging around with her either.

DANA: But she seems nice, she's been really friendly.

ANNA: Look, if I were you I'd just stay away from her and do what Sophie says for a while, then everything'll be all right.

DANA: *(nervously)* What will I have to do?

ANNA: Just stay away from Natalie. *(brightly)* It's my birthday on Saturday. I'm having a party ... I've invited most of the class. All except Natalie. You can come. Mum said one more won't matter.

DANA: But, what about Sophie?

ANNA: She'll be fine, as long as you do what she says.

(sound effect: school bell)

ANNA: *(getting up)* See you in class.

SCENE 4

(Dana enters the classroom. There's an empty seat next to Sophie. Dana walks over to it.)

SOPHIE: *(glaring up at Dana)* Sorry ... this seat's taken.

DANA: *(quietly)* But nobody's sitting here.

(Anna comes in.)

SOPHIE: Anna, saved you a place!

ANNA: Thanks, Sophie.

(Anna pushes Dana out of the way and sits down.)

SOPHIE: *(to Dana)* Natalie's place at the back of the room's empty. Sit at the back and we won't smell you.

DANA: I don't –

JADE: If Sophie says you smell, you do! Right?

DANA: Anna, I … I …

(Anna ignores her. Dana walks slowly over to the empty seat at the back of the class.)

JADE: *(loudly)* Don't you want to say something, Anna?

(Anna hesitates and Sophie nudges her sharply.)

ANNA: *(to Dana)* About my party … I've – er – I've changed my mind ... We don't want any nerds at my place. You're off the guest list.

DANA: Anna, why are you ...? Before, in the playground, you –

ANNA: Get lost, loser ... I don't know what you're talking about.

(The class laugh.)

SCENE 5

(It's art class and everyone's working on their collages.)

MRS CROXLEY: Can I see all your artwork? Remember, some of this was homework.

JADE: *(to Sophie)* I haven't bothered to do much yet. Have you?

SOPHIE: Not a lot!

MRS CROXLEY: *(loudly)* Well done, Dana! This looks really exciting, you've obviously worked really hard. *(to the class)* I wish you'd all worked as hard as Dana.

(Sophie, Jade and Anna groan.)

SCENE 6

(It's the day before the art competition. Dana's in the classroom. She has her artwork in a neat folder. Sophie, Jade and Anna are crowding around her.)

SOPHIE: *(in a sweet, friendly voice)* What have you done for the art competition, Dana?

DANA: *(nervously)* It's my street.

SOPHIE: Let's have a look.

(Dana unzips her folder and takes out her collage.)

JADE: *(surprised)* Wow! That's good.

ANNA: Doesn't look as if you'll win the competition this year, Sophie. It looks like Dana might win.

SOPHIE: *(glaring at Anna)* We'll see about that! You know what we did to Natalie's work last year.

JADE: *(to Dana)* Sophie *always* wins the art competition, don't you, Sophie?

SOPHIE: Always! One way or another, I'm the best artist in the school.

(Jade and Anna laugh.)

ANNA: Now *you* have to show up with some clever artwork.

SOPHIE: *(speaking in a sweet voice)* You want to be part of our gang? You want to be part of this place?

(Dana nods.)

SOPHIE: Then here's a little test for you. Take your collage out of the folder and ... rip it up, in front of us. Do it now. Let us see that it's ruined.

DANA: *(tearfully)* But ... I've spent ages on this. I've worked most evenings.

SOPHIE: If I win the competition ... you can join us. You can sit next to Jade in class. *(in a sugary voice)* We just want one little thing from you ...

ANNA: Just one favour.

(Dana starts to unzip her folder.)

SOPHIE: Good girl.

(Dana bites her lip and tucks her folder tight under her arm.)

JADE: What are you doing?

DANA: I worked hard on my project. I'm handing it in first thing tomorrow.

SOPHIE: *(winking at Jade and Anna)* It's too good. Your mum helped. We're telling.

DANA: You've been horrible to me since I came to this school. I don't want to be your friend. I just want you to leave me alone.

JADE: Fine, but you'll always be alone. What we say goes in this class.

DANA: *(bitterly)* I've tried to be your friend but you're not worth having as friends.

(Dana walks off.)

SOPHIE: Just like Natalie.

(Jade laughs.)

ANNA: What are we going to do, Sophie? Looks like Dana will win the art competition. Isn't there a good prize this year?

SOPHIE: *(sharply)* Shut up, Anna ... I need to think.

SCENE 7

(School's just ended. In the toilets, Dana's washing her hands in a washbasin. The folder's on top of the next washbasin. Sophie, Jade and Anna walk into the toilets. They're smiling but their smiles are unfriendly.)

SOPHIE: Hi, Dana. Still got that art folder?

(Jade grabs the folder.)

DANA: *(to Jade)* Give me that folder or ... or ...

JADE: *(to Dana)* Or what?

(Sophie grabs the folder from Jade, unzips it, pulls out the collage and deliberately tears it up. She drops the pieces onto the floor and grinds them into the dirt with her foot.)

DANA: *(pushing Sophie)* How dare you!

SOPHIE: *(mocking)* How dare you.

DANA: *(grabbing hold of Sophie's arm)* You're just a nasty bully.

(Jade pushes Dana away and Sophie trips her. Dana falls on to the floor, hitting her head on the basin. She lies motionless, blood oozing out of a gash on her forehead.)

SOPHIE: *(panicking)* Come on girls, let's get out of here.

ANNA: *(points at Dana)* But ...

SOPHIE: Let's scram ... we don't want to get caught do we?

ANNA: We can't just leave her, Sophie, we can't – Jade?

SOPHIE: Yes we can. I can. You always were too soft, Anna. Come on, Jade.

ANNA: Jade?

JADE: *(shrugging)* Sorry, but I don't want to get into trouble – do you?

(Sophie and Jade run out of the toilets. Anna waits, thinking, and then turns and runs out after them.)

(Natalie sees the girls running out and dashes into the toilets.)

NATALIE: Dana? Hold on, Dana … Oh no, they've gone too far this time. Dana, Dana, I'll get some help.

(Natalie rushes out. She quickly returns with Mrs Croxley, who crouches next to Dana.)

MRS CROXLEY: It's all right, Dana. You'll be fine.
(to Natalie) Quickly, fetch some damp paper towels.

NATALIE: Yes, Miss.

MRS CROXLEY: Dana, can you hear me? Dana?

(Natalie passes the wet towels to Mrs Croxley. She wipes Dana's forehead and Dana starts to come round.)

MRS CROXLEY: *(to Dana)* Do you think you can stand?

DANA: *(weak and shaken)* Think so, Miss.

MRS CROXLEY: *(helping Dana to her feet)* Good. We'll get you into my office and you can tell me what happened.

SCENE 8

(Natalie and Dana are in Dana's bedroom, sitting on her bed.)

NATALIE: So, you're sure you're OK?

DANA: Yes, I'm fine. Though I'm not looking forward to going back to school.

NATALIE: Well, we don't have to worry about Sophie any more. I hear she's going to another school. You should hand your artwork in now.

DANA: Really? She's going? Well, my project's ruined, but you could hand yours in.

NATALIE: *(shrugging)* What's the point? I haven't finished it. I kind of gave up after last year, and it's too late now.

DANA: What if we work on it together?

NATALIE: Are you sure you're up to it?

DANA: Definitely. Come on, we'll do the best project yet, and I've got a feeling Anna and Jade won't be so bad with Sophie gone. Who knows, we might even win!

Sophie's rules

Dana follows Sophie's rules

DANA: I don't *have* to do drama.

DANA: That's cool. I like talking too. I like fashion.

Dana breaks Sophie's rules

NATALIE: I just keep away from them - it's easier that way.
DANA: But that's not fair.

DANA: I worked hard on my project. I'm handing it in first thing tomorrow.

DANA: I don't like drama any more. I like talking about music, fashion, you know ...

(Anna ignores her. Dana walks slowly over to the empty seat.)

DANA: How dare you!

DANA: Come on, we'll do the best project yet.

Ideas for guided reading

Learning objectives: deduce characters' reasons for behaviour from their actions; comment constructively on performance; create roles showing how behaviour can be interpreted from different viewpoints

Curriculum links: Citizenship: Children's rights – human rights

Interest words: enthusiastically, smirking, appointment, motionless, collage

Resources: whiteboard, writing materials, poster paper

Getting started

This book can be read over two or more guided reading sessions.

- Explain to children that you are going to read a play about a girl starting a new school. Invite a child to read the blurb and ask children: *What might happen to the girl?*
- Discuss starting a new school. *Has anyone had to change schools? What was it like trying to make new friends? Was anyone unkind to you? How did you respond?*
- Turn to p2 and introduce the characters, deciding who in the group will read each part. Ask children to think about how they should portray the different characters, e.g. Sophie may be loud and bossy, Dana may have a gentle voice.
- Scan the first scene together, identifying the features of playscripts, e.g. stage directions.

Reading and responding

- Ask children to read Scene 1 together in their chosen parts. Give constructive feedback on the tone and pace of the children's reading and how they have portrayed the individual characters, e.g. *Good, you're making Sophie sound really angry.*
- Read through until Scene 2 and then stop to discuss questions the children have about the characters and the way they behave.